HONEY BUTTER AT THE HILL

Inn Vermont Cozy Mysteries, Book 2

THEA CAMBERT

Summer Prescott Books Publishing

Chapter One

I don't know whether you've ever been to the Green Mountains of Vermont in February, but just in case you haven't, I can describe it to you in one word. *Cold*. At least that's the word that came to mind on one particularly chilly February morning, as I woke to find that even though the little heating/ac unit in my cottage behind the inn was working its tail off, it couldn't manage to get the room up to an acceptable temperature. And by acceptable, I mean warm enough to get out of bed and hotfoot it to the bathroom, where I could then turn the hot water on full-force, and proceed to wait an eternity until it became warm enough for me to actually disrobe and get into the shower.

However, all that said, I would not dissuade anyone from visiting Vermont in February—and in fact, that was exactly what was at the forefront of my mind that chilly day. . . Right behind the concern about the mammoth goosebumps that were rising up all over my skin.

The truth is, once you're layered up in sweaters and mittens and caps, Vermont truly is a winter play-ground paradise. And as co-innkeepers, it is very important to me and my mother to let people know that we're open for business—even more so when the snow is thick and the ice on the lake is solid as a rock, and some tourists might think it too frigid to venture out away from home.

Visitors to our inn—the Inn at Pumpkin Hill—can enjoy snowshoeing, sledding, ice skating, shopping, and dining right in the heart of Williamsbridge. And since the town lies snug in the Green Mountains, cross country skiing, ice fishing, and hiking through the snowy woods are only a short drive away. Back at the inn, Mom and I are always ready for our guests to return from their adventures with hot drinks and warm cookies.

Our problem that year—our nagging problem—was

that the inn had made the news, both locally and around the state, for a little incident that happened in December, when we'd hosted an ill-fated family reunion where one of the guests was murdered. Whoever said that bad press is better than no press at all was *not* in the innkeeping business.

I'd grown up in Williamsbridge—had actually lived in the inn all my life. I went away to college, of course. Earned my master's degree in journalism, and now split my time between co-managing the inn with my mother and writing for the local newspaper, the *Williamsbridge Onlooker*. The townsfolk see me as mild-mannered innkeeper and ace reporter Eloise Lewis—but they *don't* know I am also the popular advice columnist, Miss Smithers. Technically, I'm the *fourth* Miss Smithers. I took the post after the third Miss Smithers, Edna Hillsborough, decided to retire at seventy and follow her dream of owning her own soup restaurant. Yep, Edna owns Potbelly's Soup Kitchen over on High Street, and the soup there is like nothing you've ever tasted before. Who knew soup could be so exciting? Anyway, no one knows I'm Miss Smithers other than my editor, Walter Wright—not my mom, not even Edna.

By the time I got out of the shower that morning,

somewhat thawed out and dressed in my usual layers of clothing, I headed out the door of my cottage—a (sort of) renovated caretaker's home on the grounds of the inn—and trudged through knee-deep snow to the backdoor of the main house. It was a Monday, so our weekend guests—well, our one weekend guest—had gone home the day before, and I found Mom sitting at the kitchen table with our dear friend Dr. Ian Jenkins. The two of them were drinking coffee and reading that day's edition of the *Onlooker* and laughing their heads off about something.

"Crossword puzzle got you in stitches again?" I asked, pouring myself a cup of coffee and adding a generous measure of vanilla creamer.

"The crossword puzzle?" said Doc. "Who laughs at the crossword puzzle?"

"You two do," I said, taking the seat across from Doc. "Remember last week?"

"Oh, that's right," said Mom with a giggle. "Remember, Ian? We were looking for a seven-letter word for a Vermont fish that began with W—"

"And it turned out to be *Walleye*," said Doc, laughing so hard his eyes started to water.

I sat across the table, I'm sure with a blank expression on my face. "I don't get it. Why is that funny?"

"Because of the time we went fishing as kids," said Mom.

"That's right," said Doc. "It was me, and June" —he motioned over at Mom—"and your dad. It's a long story, but needless to say, your mom ended up holding the line, and your dad and I ended up in the water."

"We did catch a walleye that day, though," added Mom.

I grinned at them as they looked at each other and burst out laughing yet again. "So," I said over the racket, "sometimes the crossword puzzle *is* pretty funny."

Doc wiped his eyes, still smiling. "That's not what we're laughing about today, though."

"It's not?" I asked, peering at the paper and wondering what page they were on. I hoped they weren't finding humor in my latest hard-hitting article about the dangers of hypothermia in February. I used to be strictly a features writer, but my editor, Walter, had been expanding my assignments of late, and to tell the truth, it might have been a blessing in disguise that we had no business at the inn. That left me plenty of time to help cover the news while still writing up features and doling out sage advice. On the other hand, the thought of losing the inn—of not being able to keep it viable—was unthinkable.

"No," said Mom. "We were just reading today's Miss Smithers column."

My heart dropped into my stomach. "Oh really?" I stirred my coffee rapidly. "And that's funny because . . ."

"Well, she answered a question about how to convince your child to eat more vegetables." Mom snickered yet again.

"What's. So. Funny?"

"She encourages parents to have a serious talk about nutrition with their children," said Doc.

"And that's hilarious because . . ."

"Oh, it's not really, dear," said Mom. "It's just that we tried that with you when you were five."

"You and Dad?"

"Nope. Me and Doc, here." Mom smiled at Doc and for the first time, I noticed she was glowing. I'm talking about the telltale glow—the one you're supposed to get when you're . . . in love.

"It was in the spring, I remember," said Doc, smiling kindly over at me. "I was just getting my practice going. You were in my office for your annual well-child checkup. Your parents were concerned about nutrition, and your tendency to eat too many sweets—"

"I stand by that tendency now, even at the age of twenty-seven."

"So I asked Doc to help me convince you to eat more vegetables—" said Mom.

"And you asked if candy corn was considered a vegetable."

"You were so precious."

Well, at least they weren't laughing *at* Miss Smithers. Not really.

"I'd better be on my way," said Doc, standing to go. "Thanks for the coffee, June."

"Always a pleasure, Ian," Mom said with yet another smile, waving to him as he bundled up and headed out.

I think that was the first time in a long while, it had occurred to me how beautiful my mother is. She's only in her mid-fifties, and since I'm within throwing distance of thirty, the age gap between us is closing rapidly.

"Mom, we need to talk about marketing. We've really got to start attracting more guests. I've got some ideas, I—"

"Eloise, before we talk about that . . . I've been meaning—I mean, I've been wanting to ask you—to make sure that it . . . doesn't bother you, when Doctor Jenkins is here. Like he was today."

"Bother me?"

She leveled her gaze at me. "Yes, Eloise. Bother you."

"Because you and Doc are . . . getting to be such good friends?"

"We've always been good friends," Mom said. She

sighed. "Are you going to make me come right out and say it?"

"What? That you've got a boyfriend?" I couldn't help smiling. "Mom, of course I don't mind. Dad's been gone for more than three years now. You're young. I'm glad you have Doc. And somehow I think Dad would be glad, too."

Mom covered my hands with hers. "Thank you, Eloise." She stood and carried her coffee cup to the sink and rinsed it. "And he's not my boyfriend."

"More of a gentleman caller?" I teased.

"Now, about the marketing," said Mom, changing the subject with the insistence of finality in her voice.

"Good morning." Matthew Stewart—my own best friend since childhood—came into the kitchen through the backdoor, stomping the snow off his boots before entering. He peeled off his parka and gloves, but kept on the worn red baseball cap he always wears down over his perpetually rumpled brown hair. Why does 'just woke up' hair look great on men but horrible on women—or on me, at least? So unfair. Matthew slung his worn leather messenger bag over the back of the chair he always sat in at the table and poured himself some coffee.

Mom and I couldn't have made it without Matthew. He started showing up to take up the slack after Dad died, and eventually became part of our little staff. Part of our family, really, since Matthew's parents passed away and I have no siblings—and neither did my parents. Which means no cousins, aunts, uncles . . . Anyway, Matthew is our family. And we're his. He's an aspiring novelist, so the steady work at the inn—and the paycheck that goes along with that—allow him to have time and flexibility to write. He handles all kinds of maintenance and assists us with everything from taking phone calls to helping me come up with ideas to get people into the inn.

Our latest scheme that quiet winter involved a social media blitz and our *Soup With Your Sweetie* special. Matthew and I had launched it the night before, paying to boost our posts and spread them all over the region. Takers would get a double suite for the price of a single, deluxe breakfast included, and one free lunch per day at Potbelly's Soup Kitchen. Edna gave us a deal on the soup, saying the special would get new customers into her restaurant—and when a couple came in and one of them got free soup, the other would be sure to buy a bowl as well. Edna's soup is that good. I mean, she'll eventually bottle the stuff and it'll be sold all over. And don't even get me started on her gourmet crackers and homemade bread! Nothing better on a cold Vermont day!

We paired our ads about the special with glorious photos of Williamsbridge in the winter and fun ideas for things to do in town, and we secured discounts for our guests at Horse Before the Cart (Who wouldn't want a one-horse open sleigh ride through a winter wonderland?) and Sugar Tap (Where our guest would receive a free sample of handmade, melt-in-your-mouth maple sugar candy.). (Of course, Evvy Sumner, who owns the place, *always* gives visitors a free sample, but we didn't mention that.)

Matthew and I were hopeful that the Soup With Your Sweetie promo would stir up some interest, because as it stood, the next few weeks at the inn were completely empty. I mean, I could understand: If I had a choice between an inn where no one got murdered and an inn where someone got murdered . . . I would probably choose the non-murder place too.

The phone rang.

"Oh, that's probably for me," said Matthew as I rose to get it. "I'm expecting a call from Stan Hill over at the lumber place."

The 'lumber place' is Hill's Lumber and Hardware. It's been in business in Williamsbridge since the dawn of time, and one Hill or another has always run it.

But the call wasn't from Stan. It was from someone calling about our special. And before the morning was out, we'd had seven more bookings—all of them couples, taking advantage of Soup With Your Sweetie. The inn was filling up fast.

Maybe there was hope we'd stay afloat after all.

Chapter Two

✥

That ill-fated family reunion I mentioned before? It was a gathering of the Fischer family from New York, and although they'd gone away with smiles and waves and promises to return (despite the untimely death of the aunt during their stay), I knew we'd probably never see any of them again.

So, I was surprised that afternoon, as I squatted in the cold, holding a board in place on the front porch while Matthew nailed it in, when he said he'd received an email from Tinsley Fischer . . . She of the gleaming blond hair and clear blue eyes. Truth be told, Tinsley's dashing brother, Tucker, had flirted with me while they were with us. But Tucker was a little *too* dashing for me—and Matthew, for his part, had said he preferred brunettes. As a brown-haired, brown-eyed girl myself, I appreciated that. But now here he was, receiving emails from Tinsley! No doubt flirtatious emails. *Flirt* was the only language Tinsley spoke.

I'd just mentioned—as Matthew hammered away at the porch board—that I found it odd that while every booking we'd gotten since running our Soup With Your Sweetie special was for couples, we'd just gotten a booking for a single. A woman named Shirley Simmons, who would be arriving the very next day, Tuesday, and staying at least through the weekend. She thought maybe even longer.

"Why would a single person come into town on a Tuesday?" I said, looking at Matthew and wondering why he didn't seem at all perturbed by that.

"Same reason as all the couples, I guess," he said. "Shopping, dining, hiking."

"She's going to do those things all by herself?"

"Why not?"

He was right about that, of course.

"And she's staying a long time—don't you think

that's strange?" Still, nothing from Matthew. "I mean, that's going to cost her a fortune."

Matthew said I should be glad for the booking, that I'd been paranoid ever since the Fischer family debacle, and that my one experience at being an amateur detective had led me to be suspicious of everything and everybody.

I told him I hadn't even thought about the Fischers since December, and that was when he told me about Tinsley's email.

"Oh. So . . . are you going to write her back?"

"I guess so," he said, a couple of nails still between his teeth. He didn't stop what he was doing or look up at me—just said *I guess so* in the most nonchalant tone possible. Typical. "I mean, it's not polite to just leave someone hanging, you know?"

"Well, I guess not. Although the nuances of email etiquette can be confusing. Sometimes there's a fine line between polite and not-polite."

He looked at me, raised a brow, and then said, "Thanks for helping me with this. You can get in out of the cold now."

I rose as gracefully as one can when one's foot has fallen asleep from squatting at sub-zero temperatures and went inside. I found Mom in the kitchen, baking a fresh batch of her almond biscotti for the upcoming weekend.

"Oh, good," she said, seeing me. "Can you hand me that bag of blanched almonds?"

I got the bag from the counter and handed it to her.

"What's wrong with you?"

"With me? Nothing!"

Mom eyed me as though she knew better. "Okay."

I flipped through the recipe file that was out on the counter. "Did Matthew tell you he heard from Tinsley Fischer?"

Mom frowned but didn't look up from her stirring. "Tinsley Fis—oh, from the Fischers who visited us in December?"

"Yes."

"She was that pretty blond girl?"

"Right."

Mom did stop stirring then, and looked at me. "Why are you gritting your teeth, Eloise? And why is your face turning red?"

I put my cold hands onto my hot cheeks. "Mom, I am not blushing. It's just—I just came in from the cold."

Mom smiled and nodded in a maddening way. "Of course, dear."

I wanted to scream, *Don't you 'of course, dear' me!*, but instead I said, "It's just that I don't think of Matthew as the emailing type. You know?"

"Well, he's a writer, Eloise. He's on that computer of his whenever he's not out working on some project for us. I don't know why you would think he's not the emailing type."

She had a point. I pressed my hands to my cheeks and cursed them. They still felt warm.

Chapter Three

It's an interesting thing, being an incognito advice columnist in a very small town where everyone knows everybody. It's like having a one-way window into your community, and no one knows it's you, watching from the other side. I can sometimes guess who it is writing to Miss Smithers, but other times, I have no clue.

For example, when I recently received a note written all in curly letters, smelling like rose perfume, and asking Miss Smithers what to do when one suspects one's husband resents one's power, it didn't take a genius to figure out that the note had come from our beloved mayor, Dory Wiggins. And trust me, her husband Lloyd does not resent her power. He just wants to spend more quality time with her.

Then again, last week I got a letter asking Miss Smithers what to do about getting along with unreasonable family members. The letter was printed out from a computer, the issue just vague enough that it could be anyone's family. And it was signed *Family Feud Fiasco*. I advised the sender to consider bringing a third, disinterested party into the mix to act as a mediator. Let's face it, sometimes you can't see the forest for the trees when you're in the thick of family conflicts. I had to wonder, as I moved around the streets of my hometown, which family was having troubles. But lately I'd been busy enough, between running an inn and my journalism work, that I probably wasn't watching people as closely as I had in the past.

On Tuesday at noon, the single person we'd been expecting arrived right on time for check-in at the inn. No matter what Matthew said, my suspicions were instantly confirmed—this guest was unusual. Her name was Shirley Simmons, and from the moment she breezed in through the front door, I could sense it: this would be one of *those* customers.

At the Inn at Pumpkin Hill, we're pretty easygoing. We meet all kinds of people and welcome them all. But once in a while, we get a particularly persnickety guest. Shirley Simmons gave herself away when she informed me that she would 'take tea' in her room each morning, rather than in the dining room. That was fine by me—we could certainly carry a cup of tea up to her room. But there was something in the way she looked at me when imparting this information . . . something inherently snooty. She wasn't a tall woman, yet somehow, she was looking down at me.

However, I gave her the key to Room 5 and she proceeded up the stairs. Without her luggage. She did pause once on the staircase and say, "You'll bring those along?" to which I answered, "Of course."

"I'll ring for the bellhop," I mumbled under my breath as I lugged the heavy cases upstairs. Once I'd returned to the front desk, the phone rang. It was Edna Hillsborough, returning my call. "Thanks for calling me back, Edna. We've had quite a few bookings for the special, and I just wanted to give you our guest count for this weekend, so you'll know how many to expect at Potbelly's."

"Oh, okay," said Edna.

Normally, Edna would have a smile in her voice and say something like, "That's great! Lay it on me, Eloise." But that day, she sounded distracted.

"You sound distracted," I said. "Everything okay?"

There was a pause. "Well, actually, could you stop by the restaurant? There's something I want to ask you."

"Of course," I said. "It's lunchtime. How about I pick up soup for Mom, Matthew, and me? Bag three of your lunch specials, okay? I can be there in a few minutes."

I got off the phone, told Mom where I was going, checked on Matthew, who was still out working in the cold, and jumped into the inn's jeep. Three minutes later, I was down the hill and on High Street, parking in front of Potbelly's. The bells above the door jingled as I entered.

"Hi, Edna," I said, heading for the counter.

"Oh, Eloise. I'm glad you're here." Edna turned around to the prep counter and grabbed a large, brown paper bag and set it in front of me. "The special today is the Vermont cheddar. I added extra bread in the bag—I know how Matthew can put it away."

Edna makes these amazing rolls and mini loaves of bread in different flavors. There's a crusty ciabatta, a mustard-cheddar loaf, dill-sea salt, sourdough, and my favorite, honey-butter yeast rolls. I've seriously considered—if I ever get married—forgoing a cake and just having tier upon tier of honey-butter rolls instead.

"Thanks, Edna," I said, handing her my credit card. "You're the best."

She took the card.

"What was it you wanted to talk to me about?" I used to live in the little apartment above Edna's garage, before I moved into the caretaker's cottage at the inn, and Edna and I had become great friends during that time. Usually, when she needed to confide something, it was along the lines of whether I thought she should wear this or that, or what color I thought she should paint her house, or which menu design I liked best.

Today, though, Edna looked very troubled indeed.

"It's a family conflict," she finally said. "I've been

having some . . . issues with a cousin of mine. It was bad enough when she was calling and emailing. But now she's actually come to town." She sighed and looked at me. "You've probably met her by now. She's staying up on Pumpkin Hill."

"Shirley Simmons?" I didn't mean to blurt it out, but the thought that snooty Shirley could be any relation of dear, kind, mild-mannered Edna was shocking.

"That's her," said Edna, looking at me with a sort of knowing look—as if she could read my thoughts about Shirley.

"So, what's the problem?" I asked.

"You know the cookbook I've been working on?"

"*Soup Every Day*? Of course," I said.

"Well, in the book are quite a few old family recipes. Everyone in our family has made them for forever. They've been passed down and improved through the years."

"That makes sense . . ."

"Well, since some of the recipes, in my thinking, belong to the whole family, I decided to share a portion of the proceeds from the book with the family."

"That's very generous of you, Edna."

"But Shirley doesn't think so," said Edna, her sweet face clouding over. "Shirley claims that several of the recipes in the book are mostly hers, and says she wants at least half the profits *plus* a cut of what I earn here in my restaurant. To make matters worse, she stopped in today before going up to the inn to check in, and saw how crowded it was. You and I both know that the special we're running along with all the extra advertising is the reason business has picked up lately, and that winter is far busier than the other seasons. But Shirley is under the impression that it's this busy year-round, seven days a week, and that I'm some kind of millionaire—making a fortune off what she thinks of as h*er* recipes."

"Oh, my." I honestly didn't know how to respond to such a preposterous notion.

"I know!" said Edna. "Shirley actually had the nerve to say that *I'm* the greedy one and that she needs the money—that I'm being selfish!" She sniffled and reached for a tissue from the box on the counter. She looked back at me with teary eyes. "I needed to talk to someone about this—someone who's outside my family, who might be able to discuss the matter . . ."

"Oh. Like a disinterested third party. A mediator," I said, realizing who *Family Feud Fiasco* might possibly be.

"That's exactly what Miss Smithers advised," said Edna, looking at me with shrewd eyes.

I felt my cheeks getting warm. "Oh, really?" I chuckled casually and added a note of lighthearted humor to my voice. "That Miss Smithers."

"Don't take this the wrong way, Eloise," said Edna with a sigh, "but I almost wish we hadn't run this Soup With Your Sweetie special together. If we hadn't been plastered all over social media, maybe Shirley never would've gotten the idea to come to town, and she never would've gotten the impression that I'm making a fortune here. I mean, it's not as though the two of us are normally in touch outside of the occasional Christmas card. I haven't even seen her for years." She sighed. "We had a falling out some time ago. Long story. But now she's got it in her head that I'm a multimillionaire with some kind of soup empire—and she wants a piece of it. A *big* piece. What am I going to do?"

"I'm not sure," I said, reaching across the counter to give Edna's arm a squeeze. "But I'll do whatever I can to help."

Chapter Four

Usually, when I return from a run to town with a bag of good food, Matthew and Mom are already sitting at the table. Our normal lunches are leftovers or sandwiches we throw together when our stomachs start to growl. Takeout is a special treat.

But today, the kitchen was empty. I could hear people moving around upstairs—not a surprise, since the inn was now half-full. I went about setting the table and placed the bag from Potbelly's in the center. Then I swung by the front desk, which is in the room just inside the long front porch that runs the entire length of the face of the inn. I was pleased to see that we'd gotten yet another booking for the Soup With Your Sweetie special for the following weekend. I answered a call for Matthew from Stan over at the lumber place, but couldn't find Matthew out in the yard, so had to take a message. *Where were Mom and Matthew?*

Just as I was about to go upstairs to look, they both came down. Mom was carrying her cleaning caddy, and Matthew had the cordless vacuum and wet-jet mop. I could tell by the look on my mother's face that something was up. We all went into the kitchen, out of the earshot of our guests.

"I have never in my life met such a disagreeable person!" said Mom, shaking her head and putting the caddy into the broom closet.

"Me neither," said Matthew, snapping the vacuum into its charger.

"Who are you talking about?" I had a feeling I already knew.

Mom gritted her teeth and lowered her voice. "That Shirley Simmons. We've just come from cleaning her room a second time, *while she watched* to make sure we didn't miss a spot. Can you believe that?"

"She had the nerve to run her finger along the top of a doorframe!" said Matthew.

"I'm so sorry I wasn't here," I said.

"Oh, don't worry," said Mom. "I'm sure you'll have plenty of opportunities to look after her during her stay. Plus, she ordered us to change the sheets *every* day."

"I actually caught the woman annoying some of the other guests," said Matthew. "She had the audacity to peek into Room 7 where that nice couple from Maine is staying. I was helping them carry their shopping bags upstairs. Shirley complained that their room is bigger than hers."

"And then, she very loudly pronounced that she's being cheated, because she doesn't get a free entrée at Potbelly's. She also went on about not getting the free deluxe breakfast. Apparently the continental breakfast that comes with her room isn't good enough, and she 'certainly isn't paying extra for a scrambled egg.'" Mom scoffed. "I told her she can have the deluxe breakfast and a gift card to Potbelly's, because we want our guests to be happy."

"And I told her that her room is smaller because it's a

single—not a double," said Matthew. "She said she should have gotten a bigger room all the same, and shouldn't be penalized because she's only one person."

Mom made a sort of 'pfffft' sound. "Thank the good Lord there's only one of her!"

"*And* that it's just for a few days," I said, unloading the Potbelly's bag.

Mom made the disgusted sound again. "A few days? She's staying for at least a week, maybe longer. That's what she told me this morning."

"And if she ever calls again, we'll say we're booked solid," I concluded.

Mom and Matthew washed their hands and came to sit at the kitchen table.

"It's Vermont cheddar soup day?" said Matthew, uncovering one of the three containers of soup. "Oh, this makes it all worth it."

"And Edna added extra bread especially for you," I said, handing out the spoons.

"Edna is the best," said Matthew, taking a bite of the

still-steaming soup and closing his eyes with pleasure. "You know, soup really is good food."

"So they say." I gave him a smirk and unwrapped a honey-butter roll and took a bite. "You're never going to believe this," I said through the delicious crumbs. "Shirley? She's, uh, Edna's cousin."

Mom and Matthew both froze and looked at me.

"Edna's—*our* Edna, you mean?" asked Mom.

"As in, the person-who-made-this-meal Edna?" asked Matthew.

"Yup."

"How is that possible?" Mom looked down as if she was asking the soup this question.

"I honestly can't imagine. But trouble's brewing in that family."

Chapter Five

But even when families are dysfunctional, or nutty, or noisy, they're still families. Back in December, when the rather large Fischer family had filled our entire inn, a switch had been flipped somewhere in my head, or in my heart. I'd realized that some part of me still longed for cousins and aunts and uncles and nieces and nephews. People to send Christmas cards to. People to roast a turkey with on Thanksgiving. Or have a potluck dinner with—where some kooky uncle brings his special Jell-O salad, and some aunt brings her signature potato casserole.

I had come to the conclusion that my family—in addition to Mom—is made up of friends and neighbors here in Williamsbridge. Like my godmother and Mom's best friend, Evvy Sumner—who owns Sugar Tap and sells all things maple sugar. Or old Noah Smith, who still works at our train station after all these years. Or Maude Hammish, who owns Suds, our gourmet soap store. Doc Jenkins. Edna. And of course, Matthew. These dear souls make up my family.

But even though I am the only child of two only children, I still sometimes wonder about my other, more distant family, out there somewhere, going about their lives, not knowing that Mom and I are here.

I was pondering all of this once again that Friday, as Mom and I tidied the kitchen and set about our afternoon chores. Matthew had gone to town to run errands, and our guests—some of whom had just checked in that day—were out doing touristy things. We'd set the Bakers up with a horse-drawn carriage ride through town and dinner reservations at the Duck and Pheasant—the village's most hoity-toity restaurant. We'd arranged a snowshoe hike through the park for the Fennells, followed by a visit to Sugar Tap, where Evvy would show them her maple trees and offer up those complimentary samples of pure maple sugar confections. Several other couples were headed out to Black Bear Mountain, to hike the trails and marvel at the beauty of the Green Mountains. Then they'd come back to town and warm up with hot drinks at the New Leaf Tea House.

We weren't sure where the lovely Shirley Simmons had gone—and I feared she'd gone back over to Potbelly's to badger Edna some more, as she did every day—but we were glad she wasn't at the inn for the time being.

Once Mom and I had scurried through the inn, tidying the common areas, turning down the beds for the evening, setting out chocolate chip cookies in the family room, and stoking up the fire in our huge stone fireplace, we took advantage of the quiet half hour by sitting down on the couch with steaming cups of Earl Grey.

"I've been thinking," I said, turning to Mom.

She took a sip of her tea. "Yes?"

"Wondering, really . . . About our family."

"Or the lack thereof?" Mom smiled her knowing smile.

"Are you sure you have no living relatives, Mom?

Not anywhere?"

"I am," said Mom, nodding. "My parents didn't have siblings. My grandparents did, but they've all passed on." She paused and looked at the fire. "You are the end of my family line." She shifted her gaze to me. "But of course, you'll probably have children someday."

I rolled my eyes. "Mom, you know I want children. But I probably ought to find a husband first."

"Don't look too hard, dear." She chuckled softly. "Sometimes the *one* is closer than you think."

"What about Dad's family?"

"You mean your dad's long-lost relatives?"

"Are there any?"

Mom smiled at me. "You remind me so much of him."

"Of Dad?"

She nodded. "He had the same thoughts, the same questions, as you. He wondered about his extended family. He'd actually started to search for them."

"Really? He never told me that."

"It was a while back, and he never contacted any of them. I thought about getting in touch with them after he'd died, but it seemed a strange thing to do. After all, it wasn't as if they'd ever met. They're distant relatives."

"So, you mean you have names? Contact information?"

"I do. Would you like to try to get in touch with them?"

"Yes! Are you kidding? Absolutely!"

She pressed my hand. "I'll get you your dad's notes. But Eloise, I don't want you to be disappointed if they don't respond. Okay?"

I was already lost in thoughts of how I would send postcards to my family—postcards of our beautiful Williamsbridge and the inn, and how they would probably want to come and visit and get to know us. How some aunt or cousin would resemble my father . . . would have his smiling eyes or tell awful jokes just like he did.

"Okay, Eloise?" Mom's insistent tone popped the happy thought bubble.

"Absolutely."

Chapter Six

"Things are getting out of hand. Can you come over?"

It was Edna. And she sounded very upset.

"Of course. I'll be right down." Since it was early evening now, the inn was still in its pre-night phase. Around eight or nine o'clock—sometimes even a bit later—our guests generally trickle back in after their days of shopping and sightseeing. They come back, full from dinner, content from exertion, and ready to sit by the fire with a mug of Mom's hot chocolate. We usually open up the wardrobe that houses our television and play movies in the cozy family room, which has both the huge stone fireplace with its comfy couches and chairs, and a dining area at the other end, just outside the kitchen. In the evenings, we set the little dining tables up with plenty of board games and put cookies and cocoa, along with hot water and a selection of teas from the New Leaf Tea House, out on the buffet.

I was surprised to hear from Edna at that time of the evening on a Friday, because Potbelly's usually had a dinner crowd—even when we weren't running a soup special together. Weekend tourists had arrived by then, and in the winter, everyone from near and far was craving hot soup. I told Mom where I was going and hopped in the jeep to head into town.

When I arrived at Potbelly's, I spotted Shirley Simmons, sitting at a corner table, hunched over a cup of coffee and a pad of paper. She looked like she was concentrating very hard on her work. Then I caught sight of Edna, standing behind the counter, stirring a huge pot of soup and glaring at Shirley. I hurried over to her.

"She's been here all day, every day, since she arrived in town," Edna said under her breath as soon as I came near.

"Seriously?"

Edna nodded. "I don't know how much more of this I can stand."

"She's driving us nuts at the inn, too," I said. "She's even managed to annoy some of our other guests."

"Oh, that doesn't surprise me one bit." If Edna could've made daggers or deadly laser beams shoot out of her eyes at that moment, I was very sure she would've.

"What's she doing over there, anyway?" I asked.

"Counting."

"Counting?"

Edna gave a quick, disgusted nod. "She's counting customers. She's taking notes on what they're ordering. Like I said, she's under the impression that it's this busy year-round. So she's sitting there, counting and calculating."

"And drinking coffee."

"And eating everything in sight."

Shirley suddenly looked up from her notes and we quickly looked away in different directions. But in the side of my eye, I could see Shirley shake her head, stand up, and walk in our direction.

"More coffee?" asked Edna, a slight quiver in her voice which I suspected was the result of her trying to keep her temper in check.

"Thanks, but no," said Shirley. "I want to talk business with you, Edna."

Edna paused, a long, thin sigh escaping her lungs.

Good for you with the deep breathing, Edna, I thought. *Way to keep from blowing up!*

"Well, Shirley, my business is really none of your business, so I can't imagine what you want to talk about." Edna's tone was measured and calm.

"That's just it, cousin," said Shirley, making the word 'cousin' sound a little slimy. "I believe your business *is* my business. You are, after all, using *our* grandmother's recipes to make the soup you're feeding all of these good people." She swept an arm across the expanse of the dining room, where every table, at that moment, was full—many of them with our guests from the inn who were taking advantage of the special.

I felt a sudden wave of guilt about that. "You should know—" I started to say.

"I have calculated exactly how much money you make in a year's time, Edna," said Shirley.

"I think we should discuss this with a disinterested third-party mediator!" Edna blurted out, turning pink all the way to the tips of her ears. Then Edna looked at me, and back at Shirley.

Shirley looked at Edna, then at me. The expression on her face clearly said, *You people are stark raving mad.* "No," she said, an irritating note of defiance in her voice.

"What do you mean, no?"

"You heard me. No. I will not have some mediator" —at this word she looked at me—"invade what is private family business. Besides," she now pointed at me, "*this* is clearly not a disinterested party anyway."

"Then we'll get another one! I'll hire one!"

Shirley shook her head as several of the diners looked over at us and frowned.

Edna lowered her voice. "Shirley, what is it you want from me?"

"A million dollars," Shirley said with a casual sniff.

"A—are you insane?" Edna's voice was no longer low.

Shirley held up her notepad again. "Don't think you can fool me into believing this is some kind of struggling little mom-and-pop operation here. I know how much money you're making—and you had no right to serve our secret family recipes without so much as consulting the rest of us! Those recipes do not belong to you, Edna!"

"They belong to me as much as they belong to anyone else!"

"Oh, really?" Shirley leveled an angry gaze at Edna. "Tell me, do you add smoked paprika to the lobster bisque?"

"Of course, I do. You know the recipe calls for it."

"But I bet you didn't know *I* was the one who suggested Grandma add it in. That was *my* idea. And it makes all the difference."

"And I was the one who started adding a dash of coconut milk to the butternut squash soup and topping it with toasted pecans," countered Edna. "But you don't see me putting my name on the recipe!"

"Cough it up, Edna. Stop trying to cheat me out of what is rightfully mine." Shirley took a step closer to Edna, and brought her voice down. "I'll make this simple for you," she ground out. "You can write me a check. Or you can close this place down."

"Over. My. Dead. Body." I had never seen Edna so angry before—or angry at all, really.

"Ms. Simmons," I said, trying to sound both calm and professional. "You are not taking into account the variances. This many customers, well, this is not the norm at Potbelly's. You have to consider—"

"I don't have to consider anything, Pumpkin-Hill Person! And I will thank you to mind your own business."

I know my jaw dropped when she made that remark, because a few moments later, I realized my mouth was still literally hanging open. *Pumpkin-Hill Person*? Again I wondered how it was possible that our dear Edna was related to this horrible woman.

"Don't you *dare* talk to my friend that way—" Edna started to say.

"Don't *you* dare think that you can continue to make money off of our family recipes without giving me my fair share. A million dollars, Edna. Or I swear, I'll ruin you."

Edna narrowed her eyes. "Don't you dare cross me, Shirley. I built this restaurant from the ground up. I took the risk. I did the work." She waved her ladle around wildly, flinging droplets of tomato-basil cream soup everywhere. "I make the soup! And no one—not you or anyone else—is going to ruin my business." Now Edna pointed the ladle menacingly in Shirley's face. "And if you try it, I swear, you will be sorry."

Several customers were now openly watching the drama unfold. I, personally, was speechless—and busy wiping tomato-basil cream soup off my face. That stuff stings when it gets into your eyes.

Shirley spun around and stormed out of the restaurant, knocking Matthew, who had just walked through the door, out of the way as she left.

Chapter Seven

"Let me guess," said Matthew, rubbing the shoulder Shirley had crashed into as he walked over to Edna and me. "The expressions on your faces have something to do with that Shirley woman."

"She is unbelievable," I said, still furious. I looked at Edna, who didn't look angry anymore. Worse, she looked defeated. I took her hand. "Edna, don't give up. If Shirley refuses to negotiate, we're going to fight her. She has no legal grounds—"

"But are you sure of that?" she interrupted, her voice hollow. "Maybe she does have legal grounds. I do use family recipes. I never thought anyone in the family would be anything but pleased and proud of that, but knowing my family, I should've seen this coming."

She looked down at the ladle, still in her hand. "I should've known." She looked around the place. "This restaurant . . . this is my dream. All those years of saving and scrimping. All for this." She paused, then cleared her throat and squared her shoulders. "Well, I have customers to serve. Back to work."

"You have two customers right here," said Matthew, taking out his wallet. He turned to me. "How about the soup and salad dinner special? With extra bread?"

"Sounds perfect." Sometimes Matthew really touches my heart with his kindness. I can't imagine a better friend—a better person.

"We can hang around and then Edna, when you have time, we can talk about what to do next," said Matthew. "The dinner rush is over, and the crowd is thinning out."

"Thank you, Matthew. Thank you both." Edna looked around the dining room. "Take that corner table. I'll bring your food shortly. It's on the house."

"Nope," said Matthew, laying a few bills on the counter. Then he took my hand and led me to our table, where he made a show of pulling out my chair before sitting himself.

I get confused when Matthew acts that way. We grew up together. We loved playing spy games and even had our own secret code. We can practically read each other's minds. But when I felt his warm hand taking mine . . . I hoped he couldn't read my mind at that moment. Or see in my face that he'd stirred something. I wasn't exactly sure what it was he'd stirred— it might be nothing. It might be a passing fancy, a fleeting sensation. And I wouldn't want to risk my friendship with Matthew for anything. I decided not to think about it.

Soon, it was easy not to think about it. Edna brought out two steaming bowls of French onion soup, smelling of sherry and caramelized onion, with a gooey, cheesy chunk of bread floating in the middle of each. There was also a loaf of crusty French bread and salted butter, and a fruit and cheese plate with smoked gouda and fresh strawberries. All of this, and a cozy corner table with a candle flickering at its center, would have made for a very romantic date—if this were a date. Which it wasn't. Although Matthew did pay. But still. I was sure it probably wasn't a date in his mind.

"So, Shirley is actually demanding a million dollars?

Is she insane?" Matthew ate his last bite of soup and picked up a strawberry.

"Edna says she sat here most of the day and calculated how many people came in and what they spent. The truth is, she was here during a busy week, in a busy season, partly because of the special we're running. Her calculations assume that business is always like that."

"I can't see how she could really force Shirley to pay her anything," said Matthew.

"But remember, Edna is also publishing a cookbook. And technically, those recipes don't belong solely to her. She wants me to act as a sort of mediator, but I don't feel qualified—and Shirley isn't too keen on the idea."

Edna waved at a couple of customers who were just getting up from their table. I recognized them from the inn and reminded them that there were cookies and cocoa waiting in the family room, as well as a warm fire. They thanked me and went on their way.

Edna smiled at Matthew and me as she bussed their vacated table. "What a handsome couple," she said.

"They are," I agreed.

"I didn't mean them," said Edna with a twinkle in her eye.

I quickly looked at my empty soup bowl. Then I looked at Matthew, who was also looking at his soup bowl.

"It's true," said Edna, coming and sitting down with us with a smiling sigh. "You two look right together."

"Oh, now, Edna . . ." Matthew said. "You know El and I are practically brother and sister."

I glanced at Matthew, then focused on the wedge of gouda. Then I chuckled lightly. "That's right," I said. "We're practically family."

Well done, Eloise. I didn't know why Matthew's comment had bothered me. After all, it was true. He was right.

I suddenly felt the urge to get back up the hill to the inn, where there was a huge plate of chocolate chip cookies waiting.

Chapter Eight

The next morning, I was up at dawn, hurrying to get bundled up and tromping through freshly fallen snow from my cottage to the inn. The clouds had cleared away in the pre-dawn hours, and the sun-crested mountains looked purple, with golden light above them, moving on up into deep blue at the top of the sky. The clear skies would make the nights colder, but the days would feel warmer and brighter. And with no new snow falling for a while, things would get easier. Our inn backs up to woods, and my cottage sits at the edge. That day, instead of going into the kitchen through the screened porch, I walked around the side of the big house, opened the gate in our picket fence, and went to the front yard. From there, the view is breathtaking. You can look down and see the little historic village of Williamsbridge with the snowy mountains rising up beside it. I always think it looks like a postcard from our vantage point.

Pumpkin Hill got its name for a very practical reason. In the fall, tons of pumpkins grow here. It's not a huge hill. Just steep enough that Matthew and I could sled down it on snowy days as kids—and sometimes as adults, too. The little drive winds down the hill, joining with Sugar Maple Street, which goes right to the town square. There lies the courthouse, town hall, the tiny police department, and the village park, with the beautiful Picadillee Pond at its center. This time of year, you can ice skate there. And our streets are lined with trees that turn brilliant colors come autumn, reflecting the oranges, yellows, reds, and browns of the mountains that surround us. But frankly, around late February, I start longing for the fresh golden greens of spring.

The town square is defined by four streets—as all squares are. Sugar Maple, Red Maple, Court, and High. And beyond and parallel to High Street, Cottontail Creek babbles its way through town, crossed by the locally famous landmark bridge—built by William Hadley, who founded the town in 1763. Yep, that's why we're called Williamsbridge.

Anyway, on mornings when we have guests at the inn, Mom and I rise early to get breakfast going. But lately, I've made a habit of walking around to the front of the inn to look over the village at sunrise and have a quiet moment of gratitude before going inside. I do this at least a few times every week.

That morning, I looked down the hill and saw, of all people, Edna. She was powerwalking down Sugar Maple Street. She glanced up and saw me and I waved at her.

"We're just getting breakfast going!" I called down to her. "Come in and have a cup of coffee!" I made hand motions depicting drinking, so Edna either understood me or thought I was inviting her up for an early morning cocktail. I glanced up at the darkened windows of the inn, hoping I hadn't awakened any of our guests—especially not Shirley.

Edna nodded and strutted up the hill, uncharacteristic energy in each step. She was a woman intent on burning off her frustrations, no doubt. "I'd love to come in for coffee," she said, a bit out of breath, when she arrived. "But not if I'll run into Shirley. You'll never believe what she's done now."

"Since last night?" I asked.

"Yep. You'll never believe it." Edna looked well and truly disgusted.

"We don't have guests in the kitchen. You'll be safe with me and Mom. Come on."

Edna was clearly wavering between wanting to get as far away from Shirley as possible and needing to unload. Then she nodded and followed me back through the picket fence gate to the backyard, where we went inside through the screened porch that adjoins the kitchen.

"So, tell us what's going on," I said, pouring Edna a hot cup of coffee and pointing to one of the chairs around our large kitchen island. She sat while Mom and I mixed up batter for cinnamon swirl and orange spice muffins.

"It's Shirley times five now," said Edna, cupping her hands around the hot mug. "You know my cookbook —*Soup Every Day*?"

"Of course," I said, nodding.

"It's in the final editing phases now—I just sent it back after making the changes they'd requested. It'll be published early next fall. Anyway, apparently Shirley got in touch with the rest of my family and told them that I wasn't giving them their fair share. I mean, I haven't given them anything yet, but I let everyone know after Christmas that the book would be published and that I wanted to share the proceeds with them all, in honor of our grandmother."

"What a wonderful gift," said Mom.

"You'd think," said Edna, taking a tentative sip of hot coffee. "And they were grateful. But this morning, I woke up to four angry emails from family members. They're saying they'd like me to reevaluate the sharing of the profits. They're expressing doubt that I've been fair. One went so far as to say I was cheating the family—and that my dear grandmother would be disappointed in me! Can you believe anyone would think—" Edna's voice caught in her throat. She sighed. "I thought I was doing a *good* thing. But now, it's all just one big nightmare."

"So, Shirley stirred them up," said Mom.

"And you said Shirley told you she needs money . . ." I said, pouring batter into muffin tins.

"That's what she told me," said Edna. "But it doesn't add up. Shirley was married to a wealthy man. He died not long ago and left everything to her. I may be mistaken, but I think Shirley might actually be quite wealthy."

"But if she's rich, why is she after you for every penny she can get?" I wondered.

"And worse, why is she set on making my family despise me? They went from thinking I was a generous person to a horrible one, and I haven't done anything wrong." Edna was clearly miserable.

I slid my muffins into one of our two ovens then went around the island and gave her a hug. "We're going to get to the bottom of this, Edna," I said.

Edna patted my hand. "I hope so."

When she'd finished her coffee, we listened carefully to make sure no guests were coming downstairs yet, and then Edna slipped out the door and down the hill to get started on the day's soups and breads.

As she was leaving, Matthew was pulling up in his

old red pickup. Matthew lives down High Street, in a tiny rental house. His commute to the inn is maybe five minutes by car—but in the spring, summer, and fall, when he isn't hauling anything, he walks to work.

"Morning," he said, walking up onto the front porch where I stood. "How's Edna doing today?"

We went inside, where Matthew had his morning coffee and Mom and I filled him in on Edna's status. We could hear the first guests beginning to trickle down the squeaky wooden staircase, so we loaded up the buffet with goodies and went back into the kitchen to start cleaning up.

"That Shirley is a piece of work," said Matthew, shaking his head. "Poor Edna."

"Keep your voices down, you two," said Mom. "She'll probably be in for breakfast any time now, and we can't have her overhearing you."

"I wonder if Shirley really is filthy rich and just pretending to need money," I said in a loud whisper.

"Let's find out." Matthew opened his messenger bag and took out his laptop.

I sat down next to him and we spent the next hour learning all about Shirley Simmons, widow of the real estate mogul, Fred Simmons. We found his funeral announcement. He'd been a good many years older than Shirley and had passed away a couple years ago. We found Shirley's various social media pages, as well as other articles about her. It seemed her main home, in Denver, was worth several million dollars. And then there was her second home, in the Bahamas, right on the water. Shirley apparently had a penchant for taking selfies with fancy tropical drinks in hand. Made one wonder all the more why she'd come to frosty Vermont in the dead of winter to bully her cousin.

I kept stealthily checking on the supply of muffins, scones, and coffee in the dining area, watching for Shirley to come down to breakfast, thinking maybe there was a way I could approach her and get some information out of her as to why she was treating Edna so cruelly. A few hours passed—plenty of time to clean the kitchen and start a batch of cookies for the evening, check on our bookings, update our website, and set up a few more social media posts to go out over the next couple of days.

There was still no sign of Shirley. We finally cleared

up what was left of breakfast, setting aside a plate with a selection of baked goods just in case our most disagreeable guest ever deigned to get out of bed.

But as it turned out, Shirley never did come down to breakfast.

Chapter Nine

✿

"Dodged that bullet," said Matthew, as I gathered up the cleaning caddy and vacuum to head upstairs to tidy the rooms. Several of our guests had checked out that morning, so their rooms would need to be reset, and of course, we'd been ordered to clean Shirley's room every day.

"What do you mean?" I asked, as Matthew took the vacuum cleaner out of my hand and we started up the stairs together.

"The crazy lady never came down to breakfast. Did you take her her tea tray this morning?"

I froze. I *knew* I'd forgotten something. "Oh no. I can't believe this! Mom and I both forgot."

"We're in trouble now," said Matthew, peering up the staircase.

"That's probably why she didn't come to breakfast! She's furious about the tea." I glanced at my watch. "It's nearly lunchtime. I bet she's down at Edna's by now, getting all set to count customers and tally up what they're spending."

"I hope so," said Matthew, nodding. "Hurry. I'll help you clean her room before she comes back."

I smiled at Matthew and we started back up the stairs. Heaven knew he had other things to do. He had a long list of projects to attend to outside. Old houses require constant maintenance. But he was taking the time to help me. "You're a true friend," I said, and when our eyes met, we both stilled. Just for a split second. But long enough that I felt my heart begin to pound. Then I found myself wondering whether he'd answered Tinsley Fischer's email and told myself to get a grip. Matthew tapped on Shirley's door and when there was no answer, he opened it with the master key and stepped aside to let me go in first.

"Thank you, kind sir," I said with a curtsy, and then breezed past him.

"I'll vacuum if you'll do the bed," said Matthew.

"Deal." I walked through the little sitting area into the bedroom.

And found Shirley.

I jumped back. She was still in bed!

"Matthew!" I whispered. "She's still—" But then I caught sight of her face. Pale. Unmoving. Eyes open. I quickly checked for a pulse, but the coldness of her skin told me it was too late.

"Oh, my gosh," said Matthew, coming into the bedroom.

I had already whipped out my cell phone and dialed 9-1-1. Within minutes, we could hear sirens coming up the hill, and once again, I was grateful to live in a small town. Matthew stayed at the door to Shirley's room, and I ran downstairs to meet the first responders.

Our police force is basically made up of Detective Phil Dunlap and Officer Marvin Potts. There are a few part-timers down at the station as well, but when something goes wrong, you can pretty much count on Dunlap and Potts rushing to the scene. They jumped out of their police cruiser and the ambulance pulled in just behind them. Doc Jenkins had come along with the paramedics, Maude Baker and Larry—whose last name is, oddly enough, Sperry. The whole group rushed up to the front door, and I directed them upstairs and told them Matthew was waiting for them.

Meanwhile, a couple more cars pulled into the parking lot behind them, and a group of people I'd never seen before got out, looking around in confusion.

"Hello," I said, coming down the porch steps to meet them. "Sorry for the mess. We've just had a—an accident. Can I help you?"

"We'd like to check in, if you have rooms available," said a tall, well-dressed woman who looked to be the epitome of *high maintenance*. Dyed and carefully highlighted blond hair. False eyelashes applied at the outer corners of her eyes. Fresh lipstick. Designer bag.

"Oh, yes," said a second woman, stepping around the first and looking up at the inn. "This looks nice and cozy. I'm glad we're staying here instead of at Cousin Edna's, like Uncle Pete."

"Hey, we'll see if you still feel that way when it's time to pay the bill," said a tall, lanky bald man, who'd arrived in the second car and was helping a short, stout couple with their bags. "Myrna and Martin, I'm sure you'll be very comfortable here."

As it turned out, the tall bald man was the aforementioned Uncle Pete, who had apparently secured free lodgings in Edna's garage apartment (where I used to live). The two high-maintenance women who looked alike were actually twins—Cousin Joan and Cousin Jennifer. And Myrna and Martin were married— Myrna being yet another cousin. These people were Edna's family.

I did have two nice suites available, ironically qualifying these guests for the Soup With Your Sweetie special. I checked them in hurriedly and showed them to the family room, where they could warm themselves by the crackling fire. Mom immediately flew into action, making coffee and offering snacks— anything to keep everyone downstairs for the time being.

I rushed upstairs to find Matthew being questioned by the ever-vigilant Dunlap and Potts, and Shirley already loaded onto a stretcher by Larry and Maude. Doc came over and joined Matthew.

"So, there was no sign of forced entry, you say?" Dunlap asked, looking from Matthew to me.

We shook our heads in unison.

"We did wonder why Ms. Simmons never came down to breakfast this morning," I said. "But we figured she'd gone to town."

"We were coming in to clean her room and change her sheets before she returned," added Matthew.

"When had Miss, uh, Simmons arrived in town?" asked Dunlap, consulting his little notebook.

"This past Tuesday," I said, feeling it had been an age since then.

"And you were changing her sheets today?"

"And cleaning her room, yes. She requested the sheets be changed every day," I said.

"At least once a day," said Matthew.

Potts and Dunlap frowned at each other.

"Sorry to interrupt your investigation," I said. "But

there are five people down in the family room right now who are this woman's relatives. Who's going to tell them what's happened?"

Dunlap and Potts frowned at each other again. Then Dunlap nodded and said, "We'd better get down there." He hesitated and looked at Matthew. "Is Edna on the way over?"

Matthew nodded. "I called her right when you arrived. She should be here by now."

Dunlap turned to Doc. "What do you think, Doc? Natural causes?"

"I can't be sure yet," said Doc. "But I'll let you know as soon as I am." He glanced at Larry and Maude. "We'd like to get the body out of here, so best to tell the family before they see us trooping down the stairs with the stretcher."

Dunlap sighed loudly and I saw him roll his eyes. "Let's go," he said to Potts, who nodded curtly and followed him out the door.

I looked at Matthew and we exchanged an unspoken decision to follow them downstairs. When we got there, Edna had arrived and the family was talking quietly. I did overhear the words 'royalties' and 'recipes' and 'fair.' Then the short, stout lady said, "We're not angry at you, Edna. Let's just talk about this." And then Uncle Pete said, "Speak for yourself, Myrna." I was relieved that no one was shouting or overtly upset, although Uncle Pete was pacing about a little.

"I feel like I've seen him before," I whispered to Matthew.

"I thought the same thing," he answered. "Then I realized he looks like that guy from that sitcom we used to watch—the one about the family that owned the pizza place?"

"Oh, yeah! He does look like that guy!" I said, unable to remember the character's name or the name of the show, but knowing exactly who Matthew was taking about.

Detective Dunlap stepped further into the room and cleared his throat. "So, you are the family of Shirley Simmons?" he asked, again consulting his notebook.

The chatter died and all eyes turned to Dunlap.

Edna stepped forward. "Yes," she said. "What's going on, Detective?"

"Well, I'm sorry to tell you this, but Ms. Simmons is —" He paused.

"Deceased," said Potts. "She's checked into that great inn in the sky."

There was a long moment of silence as the family stared at the two of them.

"Well . . ." Edna swallowed. "What—I mean, how did she die?"

"We're not sure yet," said Dunlap. "But you can bet we won't rest until we find out."

"What are you saying?" asked Edna. She started to say something else but was cut off by Uncle Pete.

"Murder!" he yelled. Then he turned horrified eyes on Edna and pointed a boney, trembling finger at her. "And I think we all know who did it!"

"Who? Me?" asked Edna. "Are you insane, Uncle Pete? I did no such thing!"

"You had all the motive in the world," said Pete.

"Now, Pete," said Martin, standing up from the couch, where his wife, Myrna, had taken out a tissue but didn't seem to be using it to wipe away any tears.

"What?" yelled Pete. "Everyone and their dog heard Edna yesterday in the restaurant—and how she threatened Shirley!" He turned to Edna. "Why don't you do the decent thing and confess?"

"I most certainly will not," said Edna. "Because I didn't kill her!"

"*'Over my dead body.'* That's what you said, isn't it? And then you threatened her! You did it, Edna. And you know it and they"—at this word he pointed at Dunlap and Potts—"are going to prove it, so why don't you save everyone some time and just confess!"

"I was angry at her, yes," said Edna. "She was being awful. But I never said I'd kill her!"

At this, Uncle Pete scoffed. "You didn't have to."

Chapter Ten

It's not that Detective Dunlap and Officer Potts are incapable of doing their law-enforcement duties on any typical day. It's just that there's no crime to speak of in Williamsbridge. An aspiring police officer who has any interest in slapping the cuffs on someone, or using the sirens on the regular, or slamming a jail cell door shut and walking away isn't going to look for a job here.

So, while we knew Dunlap and Potts were hard at work investigating the murder of Shirley Simmons—shockingly the second murder to have taken place at our inn—Matthew and I decided to do our own investigating as well. Just as a sort of backup. We'd managed to solve the Christmas murder, so our confidence was not entirely unfounded.

The welfare of our dear friend Edna, as well as the inn's reputation, were hanging in the balance. Besides, like I said before, Matthew and I have a history of shared stealth. The Spy Game was always our favorite pastime as kids. We decided to keep our eyes open and watch Edna's family like two skeptical hawks. We still didn't even know what had killed Shirley. But we suspected foul play, because Dunlap and Potts were making the rounds—stopping by the inn regularly to ask more questions of us and Shirley's relatives.

Matthew and I had been casually questioning them ourselves whenever we got the chance over the last few days. Even though Uncle Pete was staying at Edna's, he'd come over to the inn daily to confer with the rest of the family. They, unlike Edna, were *clearly* Shirley's relatives. Very demanding with a definite air of condescension.

Mom and I kept the coffee and teapots full, and made more of the cookies the family favored. While it's never easy to work with unreasonable or rude guests, we were, frankly, grateful to have steady customers over the weekdays. By the weekend, the place would be packed.

"You know what bothers me?" said Matthew, as the two of us stood listening at the kitchen door while the family chatted around the fire in the family room.

"I bet it's the same thing that's been nagging at my thoughts," I said, looking up at him and stepping away from the door.

Uncle Pete had just been talking again about how many people had heard Edna threaten Shirley. With a lowered voice, he'd said, "Why do these hillbilly cops keep questioning all of us? I've told them again and again that Edna told Shirley she'd be sorry if she crossed her. Why is Edna not already in custody?"

I pulled Matthew into the walk-in pantry so that we could speak freely while gathering ingredients for tomorrow's scones. "How does Pete know about the threat Edna made the other night at Potbelly's?"

"That's exactly it," said Matthew. "We were both there. We heard the exchange between Shirley and Edna. Pete's got it down word-for-word. But he wasn't even there. Where is he getting that information?"

I handed him a sack of flour. "Is there any chance Pete was there? I mean, we didn't know him yet. The place was crowded. He's an indistinct kind of person. I was so focused on Edna and Shirley that I didn't really look around to see who else was there . . ."

"But I thought he didn't show up in town until Saturday, with the others—after Shirley had been murdered."

"That's what I thought too—that's probably right. But is there *any* chance we're wrong about that?"

"I'd say yes," said Matthew.

"Edna will know," I said, leading him out of the pantry and setting baking soda and sugar on the counter. "We need to run over to the restaurant and check on her anyway."

"What about the scones?" Matthew nodded at the ingredients.

"I can make those after we get back." I grabbed my coat from the pegs on the wall near the entrance to the screened porch.

"Great. Let's go."

We hopped in Matthew's truck and drove down the hill and over to Potbelly's. When we arrived, my stomach lurched. Parked right outside was the Williamsbridge police cruiser. We rushed into the restaurant just as Officer Potts had taken Edna by the arm and was leading her toward the door.

"What's happening here?" I asked, running up and barring their path.

"Step aside please, Miss Lewis," said Officer Potts.

"Edna!" I felt tears stinging my eyes as I looked at my friend, who was absolutely crestfallen.

"They think I killed Shirley," said Edna.

"But you didn't!"

"Miss Lewis, get out of my way," said Potts.

"But do we even know how Shirley died—or that she was murdered?"

"That's classified information, Miss Lewis," said Potts. "Now the detective is waiting down at the station. We'd better be—"

"Poison!" said Edna.

Potts rolled his eyes. "Now Edna—I mean, Mrs. Hillsborough—I said that information is—"

"Cyanide," said Edna. "They found it in my kitchen here." She nodded over her shoulder.

Potts sighed deeply. "We're going to need to close the place down, to do a full investigation."

"Cyanide?" I asked. "So, they think you—"

"Poisoned Shirley by putting it in the soup," said Edna. "She ate lunch and dinner here every day." She turned to Potts. "Marvin, you've known me forever. You have to believe me. I have no idea how that cyanide got into my kitchen, but I absolutely did not poison anyone!" When a few of the customers looked up from their meals in alarm, she lowered her voice. "I didn't like Shirley. But I would never have killed her. Or anyone else, for that matter."

"We'll see about that," said Potts, stepping around me and pulling Edna along with him.

"Edna, we believe you," I said.

Matthew nodded his agreement. "Don't worry. We're going to find the real killer, Edna."

"And don't let them close Potbelly's while I'm gone," said Edna. She looked back toward the kitchen, where her assistant chef, Felix Andersen nodded grimly and gave Edna an encouraging fist shake of solidarity.

"I'm afraid that's not your choice, Edna—Mrs. Hillsborough," said Potts.

"But how long would your investigation take?" I asked, hurrying around to block the door this time.

Potts didn't even venture a guess at the answer. "As long as it takes."

"But Edna has to keep her business going," I pleaded. "She has expenses. Rent, salaries, fresh ingredients that will spoil and go to waste if she has to close for days."

"Miss Lewis, get out of the way." This time Potts clearly meant it. I'd pushed too far. I stepped aside, giving Edna's arm a squeeze as she passed me. "Now let's go." Pott's flung open the door. He glanced over his shoulder. "I'll be back shortly."

"After he puts poor Edna in jail," I mumbled sadly as the door closed behind them.

"Hey, Edna," Matthew called, running and opening

the door enough to stick his head out. "How long has Uncle Pete been in town?"

Edna looked back, confused. "He arrived the same time everyone else did."

Matthew and I nodded.

"I suddenly feel very tired," I said.

Matthew put a supportive arm around me. "Let's go home."

Chapter Eleven

When we returned to Pumpkin Hill, Matthew bypassed the inn and led me around back to my cottage.

"I have baking to do," I protested.

"It can wait a little while longer," he said, that note of assurance in his voice that always made me feel better. He sat me down at my little kitchen table and put the kettle on. He knew I needed hot, sweet tea to calm my nerves.

"We have to help Edna, Matthew," I said, watching him move around the kitchen, perfectly at home there.

He poured two mugs of tea, added cream and sugar to

both, and brought them to the table. "Let's go over what we know."

"Good idea," I said, taking a sip and feeling instant comfort. "We know Shirley was poisoned. And we can safely assume she'd ingested cyanide, since the police are so certain Edna is the killer and that's the substance they found hiding in her kitchen."

Matthew nodded. "Yep. It's safe to infer that someone fed her cyanide."

"We know that the poison killed Shirley sometime between Friday evening, when we saw her at Potbelly's, and Saturday morning, when she never even got out of bed."

"So, she must've eaten the poison on Friday night?"

"I'd think so."

"And who are our suspects . . ."

"I mean, Shirley's from Colorado . . . and apparently the Bahamas . . . Locally, Edna is the only person she knew. Her family didn't arrive until after we'd found her body."

Matthew let out a long sigh. "Doesn't look good for Edna."

"Matthew! You know she didn't do it!"

He put a hand over mine. "El, of course I know she didn't do it. What I mean is, it makes perfect sense that the police are looking at Edna. She had a very strong motive."

I nodded in agreement. "Shirley was going to ruin her," I said glumly.

"And she had means."

"The cyanide in her kitchen."

"And opportunity."

"Because Shirley was at Potbelly's almost round the clock." I looked at Matthew, who looked back at me for a moment, then slipped his hand away quickly and cleared his throat. "You're right," I said. "It doesn't look good for Edna."

"But then again, it makes no sense that she'd slip cyanide into Shirley's soup and then leave it right there in her kitchen. A real killer would get rid of it. Edna's no fool."

"But there have to be other suspects. Shirley was an awful person—at least what we knew of her. And if she was awful to Edna, she was probably awful to someone else too. We just need to figure out who that is."

"I still don't understand how Uncle Pete knew about that argument between Shirley and Edna at Potbelly's. He's acting like he heard it firsthand. But he didn't get into town until the day after it happened."

I sipped my tea and mulled this over. "I guess he could've heard it from someone, somehow . . ."

"Oh—and another thing. Those twins, Edna's cousins—what are their names?"

"Joan and Jennifer?"

"Yes. I overheard them earlier, when you and your mom stepped away to prep another batch of pancakes this morning. They were asking the others how much they would get if Edna was found guilty of Shirley's murder. Pete had just accused her again, and they were wondering if the fact that Edna would be in jail would somehow translate to more money for them. Can you believe that?"

"Who *are* these people? Edna has a seriously dysfunctional family!"

"Poor Edna." Matthew sipped his tea and shook his head. "I wish we didn't have so many unanswered questions."

"Then let's revisit the only things we know for sure. Edna didn't kill Shirley Simmons. And the only way to help her is to find the real killer."

Chapter Twelve

I couldn't even begin to imagine the night Edna had spent in jail. I didn't sleep much that night either, truth be told. I kept checking in with Officer Potts and whoever else answered the phone at the police department—kept thinking they'd realize that arresting Edna had been an act of insanity and release her. But they never did. So early Tuesday morning, I was back on the phone, and was told that Edna's bail hearing had just been set for that morning at ten. Mom and I hurried through our morning chores. When Matthew arrived, he took care of a few small projects, and then we all piled into the jeep and headed down the hill to the courthouse.

Williamsbridge is the county seat, so there were

several other groups of people waiting to see Judge O'Leary. Matthew, Mom, and I found seats in the front row on the left side of the center aisle, just behind the attorney's table that faced the bench.

"Oh, I'm glad we caught you here." Joan Wilson, followed by her twin, came and sat down next to me, crossed her legs elegantly, and leaned back comfortably in her chair—as though we were all relaxing in a movie theater, waiting for the show. Myrna and Martin filed into the row behind us, along with Uncle Pete.

I turned and looked at Joan and waited for her to continue.

"It's about our room," she said.

"It's too small," said Jennifer, leaning around her.

"Do you have anything with a big screen tv?"

"And we'd really prefer a two-bedroom suite. King beds in both rooms, please."

"We, uh, don't have any two-bedroom suites," I said, pretty much dumbfounded that these women had the audacity to make these requests at this time, in this place. "You can rent a second bedroom and each have your own suite."

"Rent? Do you even think it's fair that we should be paying at all, considering our dear cousin died at your inn?" Joan asked with a huffy little sniff.

"Would we still get the special rate if we each had our own room?" Jennifer chimed in.

"Um, no, because then you'd be renting two singles . . . not one double. We aren't currently running a special for single rooms." Frankly, if the two of them weren't so snotty, I'd have gladly struck a deal with them. But they clearly didn't deserve it.

"I'm sure you'll make an exception in this case," said Joan in a tone of voice that said, *This conversation is over. Just see to it.*

I felt my cheeks burning, but before I could manage a response, Edna was brought into the courtroom by a bailiff and was seated at the table in front of our row. She turned weary eyes to look at me, but then her attorney whispered something to her and she turned back around.

The bailiff announced the case and Judge O'Leary

mulled over the papers in a file that was handed to him. He glanced at Edna.

The defense attorney stood. "Your honor, we'd like to request a lower bail. Mrs. Hillsborough is a first time offender, and—"

"Bail stands at one million dollars," said the judge, looking stern.

"But your honor—"

"This is, indeed, a first offense for Mrs. Hillsborough," the judge went on. "But the charge is murder, and there is reason to believe the defendant might run."

Edna stood up so abruptly, her chair fell over behind her. "What? Why would you think that?" she said, sounding overwrought and exhausted. "Who told you that?"

The judge pounded his gavel.

"Why are you so surprised, Edna?" Joan shouted from beside me. "You love to steal and lie! You're right where you belong!"

At this, Uncle Pete made noises of hearty approval.

The judge did not take kindly to yelling in his court-room and pounded the gavel again, then nodded to the bailiff, who took Edna's arm and escorted her out the door. She glanced back at us only once, eyes filled with tears.

I looked at Joan. I had never felt so enraged. Joan completely ignored me. She gathered her things and then turned and walked away with the rest of them.

As we trudged out of the courthouse, Matthew put a hand on my back, and I felt my anger melting into sadness. "Why would Joan say that about Edna stealing and lying? What was she talking about?"

Matthew just sighed and shook his head, clearly as dumbfounded as I was.

"We have to figure out a way to get her free," I said.

"Eloise, the police are investigating," Mom said. "I don't want you involved. Surely the true killer will come to light. Please don't forget that this business is dangerous."

As Mom moved on ahead toward the truck, I hung back slightly and gave Matthew's arm a tug.

"I know," he said, reading my thoughts. "We have to help Edna."

"I don't know how we're going to do it, but we have to do something."

"Well, in my opinion, if you want to catch a killer, you have to set a trap."

Chapter Thirteen

Back at the inn, Matthew asked me to help him clear the various paths around the mounds of snow. Pumpkin Hill Lane curves up the hill from Sugar Maple. Our gracious old inn crowns the hill, and the yard blurs into woods on three sides. The front of the inn faces to the east—toward sunrise and the village. The woods that surround the inn—keep in mind that the hill is huge and is actually more of a series of rises and falls, with us on a broad sort of plateau—gets thicker as you go further into them. My cottage is behind the inn, where the backyard meets the woods. Just beyond it, slightly further into the trees, is the old kitchen building from colonial times. Having that separate kitchen would've kept the house from overheating in the summer . . . or from catching on fire, of course, back in the day. These days, the old kitchen is empty, but charming none-theless. One day, we'll restore it, but that project is on the proverbial back burner for now. Our home has been here almost since good old William Hadley founded the town in 1763. It came into my family many genera-tions ago on my father's side, and my ancestors have restored it, updated it, gotten married in it, had babies in it, danced in it, died in it. I didn't realize until adult-hood just how blessed I was to grow up on that dear old hill, and can't imagine living anywhere else.

There are little pathways that lead, for instance, from the front parking area to the front porch steps. And from the side porch steps around to the gate in the picket fence. From the other side of the porch to the gardens—in the spring, summer, and fall, we have both cutting and kitchen gardens that also have little paths going through and around them. And of course, there are pathways around in the backyard, from the back of the inn to my cottage, to the old kitchen, and to the walking trails that lead off into the woods.

Matthew and I had our work cut out for us, clearing the snow from all of these paths, but at least the day was sunny with a peerless blue sky. After we'd been shoveling for a few minutes, he stopped.

"I've got an idea," he said.

I stopped shoveling and looked at him. Then we both glanced at the inn, where Edna's family was currently ensconced in their usual fireside chat. We looked back at each other, nodded, and walked casually over to the workshop, then ducked inside.

"What's your idea?" I whispered.

"I don't think we have to whisper in here," he said, grinning at me. "So. Edna's horrible family is counting on Edna being cut out of her own business, right?"

"Right . . ."

"They think she's the only person standing between them and the fortune they believe she's making, between the restaurant, and the upcoming book deal, and maybe even the chance to sell the soup commercially someday." He glanced at me. "You with me so far?"

"Okay . . ."

"But what if Edna had a husband?"

I snorted. "Don't you think her own family would know if she had a husband?"

"Not necessarily. After all, Edna hasn't been in touch with any of them for years."

"Can't say that I blame her for that," I said. "Go on."

"Let's talk to Walter about this. We'll—"

"Walter, as in my boss at the newspaper?"

"Yep. That Walter. We'll get him to let you write an article for the paper about this whole mess with Edna, and we'll say that Edna's husband, who's been out of the country for some time on business, is rushing home. We'll try to get this into Thursday's edition and we can say he's coming home that night."

"Walter would probably let us do that if it meant helping Edna," I said. "They're old friends, and he owes her one anyway because she lets him run a tab at Potbelly's since he's always forgetting his wallet."

"I'm glad he owes her one," said Matthew, "because we're going to need him to go one further."

I raised a brow and waited.

"He can pretend to be the husband—let's call him Mr.

Charles Hillsborough. Wait—no. Edna's family name is Hillsborough. So he'll be Charles . . . " Matthew glanced at the tools in the shop and pointed at a hack saw. "Charles Sawyer."

"Walter? Pretend to be Edna's husband?" I tried not to fall over laughing at the notion.

"Why not? He's a little younger, but he's close to the right age, and he's constantly holed up in that newspaper office, so Edna's family won't have seen him around town."

"So, we write this article and make sure they all see it. Walter pretends to be Edna's husband, Charles Sawyer. What's the trap part?"

At my question, Matthew took on a wise expression. He was eating this up. "Well, you see, I have a hunch that the killer got rid of Shirley because she was in the way. She was standing between them and Edna's purported money. So, when Mr. Charles Sawyer returns to town, that'll be just another person they need to eliminate."

I nodded, finally understanding where Matthew was coming from. "The killer has already come this far— they've already killed to get at that money. They're fully invested. They'll make a move to do away with Edna's husband, and we'll catch them in the act!"

"Exactly!" He paused. "This is assuming the murderer is one of Edna's family, of course. You think it'll work?"

"I think it's worth a try."

"What have I gotten myself into?" Walter Wright looked in horror at the wedding ring I held out to him.

"Take good care of this. It was my dad's," I said, shoving the ring at him.

He took it and slipped it onto his left ring finger. He, Matthew, and I were in his office at the newspaper.

"Besides," I said, "just think of the hard-hitting news article we're going to get out of this whole thing. You get to be an undercover reporter."

Walter sighed. "Reminds me of my younger days."

"You're about to prove to yourself that you've still got it," said Matthew.

It was Thursday—two days after Matthew and I had begun to formulate our trap. As far as we could tell, the police weren't any closer to finding the real killer and setting poor Edna free. Thursday's edition of the *Williamsbridge Onlooker* was still hot off the presses, but Edna's family had devoured it right along with their breakfast that morning. Uncle Pete had taken to helping himself to our deluxe breakfast bar, even though he wasn't a guest of the inn—which on this day, we were glad of. He'd loudly mentioned that it was a good thing he'd been staying over at Edna's garage apartment, because with her in jail, someone needed to look out for the yard and such. I wondered what there was to do in the yard in February.

"So tell me again what, exactly, I'm supposed to do," said Walter.

"Take these keys," said Matthew, handing Walter a ring with a couple of keys on it.

"These are the keys to Edna's house?" Walter asked, tucking the keys into his pocket. "Why do you even have these?" He eyed Matthew.

"Because I do odd jobs for Edna all the time," said Matthew. "She gave them to me years ago. The big one is to the house. The little one is to the garage apartment."

"All you have to do is take this suitcase"–I pointed at the empty suitcase we'd brought over—"and drive up to Edna's house tonight, get out of your car with the suitcase, and go into the house. Turn on lights, make a little noise, and then sit on the couch—do whatever a husband who's been out of town would do upon returning from a long trip."

"Okay . . ." said Walter slowly. "And when some nut from Edna's family jumps out and tries to kill me . . . what happens then?"

"We've been nagging Detective Dunlap and Officer Potts for twenty-four hours straight," said Matthew with a chuckle. "We think they've finally agreed to come with us."

"Wait. You *think*?"

"We're pretty sure they'll be there," I said.

"We'll be at Edna's hiding and ready," Matthew continued. "If the killer tries to attack you we'll grab them, and *boom*—Edna's off the hook and the real killer's off to jail."

Walter nodded. "Okay. But I'm taking my recorder and my notebook. And I'd better get a story out of this."

Matthew and I left Walter and headed back to the inn and went about our early evening routine as usual. When darkness fell, and the appointed hour was near, I grabbed my backpack and quietly slipped out of the house and ducked into Matthew's truck. He hung back for a time and then made a show of saying goodbye to Mom, who was not thrilled about our scheme but had accepted that we couldn't be deterred.

Matthew climbed into the truck, shut the door loudly, and we drove down the hill.

"The coast is clear," he said, once we'd turned onto Sugar Maple.

I came out of my hiding place in the backseat, and climbed up into the front, lugging my backpack along with me. "Good. My left foot had fallen asleep. Also, I found this under the seat." I held up a dilapidated green frisbee.

"Huh! I haven't seen that in about five years." He eyed my backpack. "What's with the bag? Did you bring snacks for our stakeout?" he teased.

"No," I answered, rolling my eyes and making a note-to-self not to share my gummy bears with him. "I have important things in here. My phone, a rope, a good camera, a flashlight—"

"A baseball bat," said Matthew, reaching over and tapping the handle of the Louisville Slugger that was sticking out of the top of the bag. "What's that for?"

"Protection."

"We won't need protection, though, because at the first sign of trouble, we turn it over to the police. Agreed?"

I sighed. "Of course."

We drove down Sugar Maple, hung a left on High Street, and were soon pulling into Matthew's drive-way. The cozy little house Matthew rents, just past the town square, is a walkable distance from Edna's house. She lives on the corner of Blue Spruce and Red Maple, just over William's Other Bridge. (Yep, that's what it's called—not to be confused with William's Bridge, further up the creek.)

We had both purposely worn dark clothes that day, and I admit that my adrenaline was high as we snuck under cover of darkness toward Edna's. It felt just like our Spy Game days. Except this was no game.

The plan was to meet Dunlap and Potts behind the little shed in Edna's yard—that is, if they decided to come. We'd encouraged them to come . . . then insisted they come . . . then sort of begged them to come. They were ardently noncommittal, and held that we should leave the investigating solely to them. Anyway, once we were all present and accounted for, we would sneak closer to the house where, thankfully, Edna has a tidy row of shrubbery right under the living room windows. Walter would arrive about ten minutes later, and then we'd watch and wait until the killer showed his- or herself—*if* they did.

Matthew and I made it to Edna's and snuck behind the shed. The night was eerily quiet and there was no sign of our friends from the police department.

"Where are they?" I asked, my heart pounding. "Walter will be pulling up any minute! What if they don't come? Or what if they come at the wrong time?"

"It'll be okay." Even in a whisper, I could hear the calm in Matthew's voice. He took my hand and I felt my shoulders drop, my jaw unclench. Matthew smiled at me, barely visible in the shadows. "This is just like when we were kids."

"Except that back then there wasn't a real killer on the loose."

He chuckled softly. "Except for that."

He still hadn't let go of my hand, I realized. I looked up at him. He looked down at me. I swear he moved a hair closer, and in that moment, I wasn't sure what to do. It was so quiet I could hear him breathing, so chilly I could feel his warmth.

That was when we heard a scuffling around the other side of the shed, and Dunlap and Potts appeared.

"Glad you decided to come," Matthew whispered, letting go of my hand.

"Walter will be here any time now," I said. "Let's move in."

"Now hold on just a minute there," said Potts. "This is where you two get off."

"What? No way," said Matthew.

"You need to leave the investigating to the police from now on," said Dunlap.

"But this trap is our idea," I said.

"And we appreciate that," said Dunlap in a tone you'd use with a five-year-old. "But we'll take it from here."

"Frankly, this is probably going to turn out to be a colossal waste of time," said Potts with a sniff.

"Then you won't mind us hanging around," said Matthew, taking my hand again and pulling me along toward the shrubbery. We stayed low to the ground and kept to the shadows. I could hear the pitter-patter of Potts and Dunlap behind us. Suddenly, headlights crossed our path and we dove into the bushes in one clump, falling onto each other as we did.

Walter had arrived. We couldn't see him from our vantage point, but we could hear his car door open and shut, hear his footsteps along the walkway and up the front steps, and then the sound of the screen door opening and the key turning in the lock and the front door opening and closing. Within a few moments, lights came on in the house and Walter had made it to the living room.

We slowly raised up enough to see him, sitting on the couch, scratching notes in his notebook. All was going to plan.

"You two really need to vamoose now," whispered Potts. "This could get dangerous, and we don't have any use for a couple of wannabe detectives."

"We're not leaving," said Matthew. "Besides, you might need us."

At this, Dunlap snorted quietly.

"Hey, we've helped you before," I reminded him.

"There's nothing more dangerous than—"

At that moment, we heard another sound. Footsteps, coming up the front walk in the darkness.

Chapter Fourteen

For a split second, I felt a sense of the hilarity of the situation. We'd gotten out of order in our rush to hide, so there I was, huddled tightly in Edna's shrubbery between Potts and Dunlap, with Matthew down at the end of our little group. None of us moved a muscle, and I realized a few seconds in that I'd been holding my breath.

We heard the footsteps pause as whoever it was reached the front door. For a moment, I thought maybe I'd imagined the whole thing, but when I looked over at Matthew and saw his eyes, unblinking and wide, I knew the ominous sound had been all too real. Goosebumps ran up my spine and I shivered, but not from the cold.

We heard the telltale squeak of the hinges on Edna's screen door. Another pause. The front doorknob turned, ever so slowly. As one, the four of us rose slightly to peek into the very bottom of the window, where a hapless Walter still sat on the sofa, engrossed in his writing.

"Go around to the side, where we can see the intruder!" hissed Dunlap.

Potts started to move.

"Not *you*!" said Dunlap. He looked at me. "You!"

"Me?"

"Her?" whispered Matthew. "Let me go. I can—"

"She's the smallest of us by far. The suspect is in the kitchen over there on the other side of the living room, I'm pretty sure. That floor-to-ceiling side window between here and the kitchen is unprotected and she's the only one who could slip under it without being seen. We only have a few seconds here. Potts, get ready to move in."

Potts gave a nod, and I couldn't tell whether he was excited or horrified.

Dunlap looked back at me. "When you get to the kitchen window, take a look and give us a thumbs up if you see anyone. If for some reason we're mistaken, I don't want to blow our cover just yet and ruin this whole sting."

I glanced over at Matthew, who looked like he was trying not to look worried. Then I crept to the side window. When I got there, I dropped to the ground and slithered along underneath it to get to the kitchen window. I peered in. A shadowy figure, wearing a hood and what appeared in profile to be a ski mask, stood in the darkened kitchen, peering into the living room. He made one slight move, and the knife in this hand glinted in the dim light and caught my eye. I looked back at Dunlap and nodded frantically, giving a thumbs up.

"Stay back," he said, and he and Potts, weapons drawn, ran to the front door, no longer worried about being seen or heard. Matthew ran over to join me at the kitchen window, where we could see the action, both inside the house and out. Dunlap turned the front doorknob, but found that the intruder had had the presence of mind to lock it behind him. "Kick it open!" he ordered, and Potts rushed at the door, kicking it wildly to no avail. He kicked it again. Then rammed it with his shoulder and grunted in pain.

I looked into the kitchen window, where the shadowy figure had obviously heard the commotion and had decided to act quickly. The knife rose in the air, and the person moved through the kitchen to where it joined the living room.

Without hesitating, I opened my bag, took out the baseball bat, and rushed to the large side window.

"El, what are you—"

The glass shattered. Matthew and I hurried in—me still wielding my trusty bat. The hooded figure turned toward us, taking his focus off Walter. At that moment, Potts and Dunlap, who'd finally managed to get in the front door, rushed into the room and were able to grab the intruder from behind.

"Freeze!" yelled Potts.

Something told me he'd always wanted to say that.

While Potts pointed the gun, Walter scurried to safety, where Matthew and I stood, and Dunlap pulled back the hood and ripped off the mask.

But it was already pretty obvious who we were dealing with. The tall, lanky frame gave him away. An angry looking Uncle Pete stood there in the middle of the living room. While Potts kept the gun poised on him, Dunlap snapped on the handcuffs and read him his rights.

As if all of that hadn't been shocking enough, Edna's other family members came in through the broken front door, which still stood ajar. Pete saw them, rolled his eyes, and plopped down onto the couch as if he just couldn't stand any longer.

"Aha!" said Joan. "We were right!"

"What are you talking about?" asked a now defeated Uncle Pete.

"We knew you killed Shirley, and we knew you were up to something tonight after being so upset about that newspaper article this morning," said Jennifer. "We were over at the inn, and the more we talked about it, the more worried we got."

"And the more we became convinced that you were Shirley's killer!" said Jennifer.

"So we decided to come over and check," said Myrna.

"And sure enough, here you are," said Martin.

"Guilty as sin," said Joan. She sidled up to Detective Dunlap and wrapped a hand around his arm. "We're so sorry, Detective. We should've told you about our suspicions sooner."

"But we didn't have the proof yet, you understand," said Jennifer, slinking over and taking his other arm.

"And then, when Pete found out Edna's married, well!" Myrtle scoffed.

"He was fit to be tied!" said Martin.

"She isn't married," said Potts. He smirked at Pete. "This was all a trap, set to catch a rat."

Pete's face turned red with rage. "It was all Shirley's idea!" he yelled. "All hers! We were supposed to get the money and split it!"

"Come on over to the station," said Detective Dunlap, prying the manicured fingers of both Jennifer and Joan off of his arms and pulling Pete to his feet. "We'd love to hear the whole story."

Chapter Fifteen

"So, Pete was in cahoots with Shirley to swindle Edna?" I asked.

It was Friday morning, and Edna, who had been released from jail late the night before when they took Pete in, had come to the inn for a celebratory breakfast, along with her family and Potts and Dunlap.

Dunlap had decided it would be simpler to take everyone's official statements at the inn, since they were all there. The real reason, of course, was that he was looking for Mom's coffee and baked goods.

"That's right," said Edna. She looked over at Detective Dunlap, who was dipping a biscotti into a cup of coffee at the moment. "Pete confessed to everything."

"But why did Shirley want your money?" I poured a cup of coffee and handed it to Matthew. "We thought she was independently wealthy."

"She was," said Edna. "Well, her husband was. When he passed away, he left very specific instructions in his will. He left his fortune to Shirley, but he put her on a strict allowance, to keep her from overspending." She looked down. "Shirley hated her husband for that, and she hated me too."

"You? Why?" I asked.

"Because I was the one who told Lyle—that was Shirley's husband—about her overspending. Many years ago, before our falling out, we'd gotten together in Denver at their estate—all of us." Edna motioned toward the rest of the family. "Shirley and I stayed up late one night. She'd had too much to drink, and spilled the whole sordid story about how she used their different charge cards and then sometimes paid for part of expensive items with cash, to make it look like she hadn't spent that much. Lyle would've figured it out on his own eventually, but he was an extremely busy man. I . . . well, I clued him in. I thought it was for Shirley's own good. She never forgave me for that."

"So, this strict allowance," Matthew said slowly, "was putting a cramp in Shirley's style."

"And she wanted to get more than her fair share of Edna's book deal," said Joan.

"And then when she saw how well the restaurant was doing, she wanted a piece of that too," added Jennifer.

"Pete loved money just like Shirley," said Marvin. "He was always scheming in one way or another, and Shirley knew it. So she told him he'd get a bigger cut of whatever she could get off of Edna if he'd help her."

"But Pete came into town with the rest of you, didn't he?" Mom asked. "And Shirley had died just before you got here."

"No, he only pretended to arrive Saturday with the rest of us. Pete had been here all week. Hiding like the rat he is," said Joan.

"Hiding where?" Matthew asked. "He certainly wouldn't have gone unnoticed in Edna's garage apartment."

"Right here at the inn," said Jennifer. "He bragged about it to us. He was sleeping on the sofa in Shirley's room. He'd sneak in and out at night and early in the morning, putting on a coat and hat whenever he was around town."

"He's a very nondescript kind of person," said Joan, inspecting her shiny red nail polish. "No one really remembers him based on looks."

Mom, Matthew, and I looked at each other. It was disconcerting, knowing a killer had been sneaking into our inn over the past week. But then again, Shirley had been the one letting him in—it wasn't as though he'd broken in. And that did explain why Pete looked familiar. We'd probably seen him in town. And Shirley was clearly the one who'd recounted her argument with Edna in such detail.

"So, Pete put the cyanide into Shirley's food?" I asked.

"This is where I take over," said Detective Dunlap, putting down his coffee and adjusting his belt. "Pete and Shirley had a scheme none of you even know about. See, they knew their chances of getting Edna to write them a check without a fight were slim. So they decided to frame her instead. Pete was in charge of the cyanide."

"A low level of cyanide in the blood won't kill you," Potts piped in. "Just make you sick. Headache. Dizziness."

"Potts, I'm telling it," said Dunlap. He cleared his throat and continued. "They were going to put a little cyanide in Shirley's drink after she'd eaten at Potbelly's, let her get the tiniest bit into her bloodstream so a blood test would affirm it, and then Pete, who was extremely good at sneaking in and out of places without being noticed, would plant the poison in Edna's kitchen. Then, they'd sue the life out of her, send her to jail, and take over the restaurant."

"They thought I was making millions because of the crowds who've been coming in recently, with the special we've been running," Edna explained.

"But Pete hated how Shirley would order him around, talk to him like he was stupid," said Dunlap. "So, after that big blow-up with Edna at Potbelly's, when Shirley had had too much to drink and was being particularly obnoxious, Pete *accidentally* put a little too much poison into her drink. He says he didn't mean to kill her—just make her sick."

"He always was the bad apple of the family," said Myrna, smoothing out her skirt.

"So, he didn't mean to kill Shirley . . ." Matthew said.

"But he was definitely planning to kill Walter," I added.

"For sure," said Joan. "If Edna was married, that would ruin everything."

"I can't wait to read the Sunday edition of the *Onlooker*," said Matthew, grinning at me.

"I've, um, brought something along with me to show you all," said Edna, opening her large tote bag. She took out a thick file and what looked like a ledger book. "I want to be very transparent with all of you, my family." She opened the file and took out several pages, arranging them in an orderly fashion on the table they all sat around. "These are my tax returns for the past few years, since I opened Potbelly's. That book shows my record of overhead expenses and profits. You can look through this file of receipts to confirm everything."

The members of Edna's family all looked surprised, but none of them reached for any of the documents.

"Go ahead," said Edna. "I want you to look at them. If you do, you'll see that I'm not a millionaire. I get by, I make a little profit . . . But the soup kitchen is my dream. I want to share our heritage with others. That's why I do it. I don't make a lot of money when all is said and done."

"But the restaurant has been so crowded," said Jennifer, leaning forward and looking over the paperwork.

"In large part because of a promotion I've been running with the inn," said Edna. "For almost every couple you see at Potbelly's, one of them is getting free soup."

"But that cuts into your profits—" Joan started to say.

"That's okay with me," said Edna with a smile. "It brings new faces into the restaurant. It makes me happy to feed them all. I decided to write the cookbook because so many people ask me for the recipes. And I'm not giving away *all* our family secrets. Just a few of them. I don't expect to make millions off of that little cookbook either, but I thought it would be a nice gesture to share whatever I do make with all of you. That's all."

Myrna picked up a document, scanned it, and set it back down. "Oh, Edna, we owe you an apology. We thought—Shirley led us to think—"

"She wound us all up," said Joan. "She got us all to buy into the story that you were the next thing to a thief." She looked down. "We shouldn't have believed her."

"Joan's right," said Myrna. "We should've trusted you, Edna. You've always been a decent person. It was just so tempting to believe Shirley, because she promised us a lot of money and turned us against you."

"We're so sorry, Edna," said Jennifer, and everyone else nodded their agreement.

Edna took a deep breath and raised her chin a little. "You're forgiven."

Everyone stood and hugged everyone else, and the chatter got pretty loud. Mom, Matthew, and I stood back to give them some space, then edged back into the kitchen so that the family could have some time together, and Dunlap and Potts could take their statements.

I felt a wash of relief for Edna. She'd managed to patch up the family—and she hadn't even needed Miss Smithers to intervene.

Chapter Sixteen

"I'm so glad everything worked out with your family." It was a few days later, and Edna and I were out for a morning walk together. Edna's no spring chicken, but she's fast! Anyway, Edna's family had left Williamsbridge on good terms—all promising they'd get together for family reunions at least once a year from then on. I felt a little pang of envy when they'd hugged and cried and laughed about old times and good recipes. They'd collectively made the decision to donate the proceeds from *Soup Every Day* to several charities dedicated to feeding the hungry.

"And we didn't even end up needing a third party," said Edna, still looking straight ahead as we turned onto Sugar Maple and headed back toward Pumpkin Hill. Then she glanced at me. "Or did we?"

I could tell by her smile that she knew. "So . . ."

"Yep. I know you're Miss Smithers."

"But how?"

"I figured it out when you mentioned using a disinterested third party to help sort out my family problems that day at Potbelly's." She smiled at my worried expression. "Don't worry, Eloise! I won't tell a soul. I'm glad you got the job after me. I was hoping Walter would give it to someone as capable as you." She linked arms with me as we started up the hill. Then she paused. "But Eloise, it truly must remain a secret. Otherwise, folks won't be comfortable around you. Everyone eventually needs the aid of Miss Smithers. It's an important responsibility you have."

I nodded. "I know. I promise I'll take it seriously."

"I know you will." She gave my arm a squeeze and we continued up the hill.

With all of our guests checked out, and the next bookings not until Thursday, we had a rare pocket of time to slow down, reset the inn, bake, and enjoy the waning winter days. The sun was shining brightly and the snow was melting—at least until the next snow-fall. One more month and spring would begin to arrive.

When Edna and I reached the top of the hill and bustled inside, we found Mom, Doc, and Matthew sitting around the fire, drinking hot chocolate. Mom poured Edna and I each a steaming mug and swirled in mounds of marshmallow cream. I had just taken my first sip when the phone rang at the front desk.

"I'll get it," I said, stepping into the next room.

The phone call wasn't a guest wanting to book a room, or even Stan over at the lumber place. It was a woman named Rebecca—and she was my cousin on Dad's side. A cousin! She said she had been so happy to receive my letter, and that she and the rest of her family would love to meet me!

"Are you serious? And they live in Maine?" Matthew asked when I told everyone about the phone call.

"Yes! On a rocky beach. Can you believe it? She says their door is always open. We're going to get to know each other through email for now, but someday, I could even go and visit them!" My heart felt like it was about to burst. I had cousins. And an aunt and uncle. And I would meet them all someday. And who knew? Maybe we'd even become great friends, spend the occasional holiday together, drop each other Christmas cards every year . . .

I was lost in thought, imagining myself strolling down the beach with my cousin Rebecca, laughing about how we looked a lot alike—maybe we both had the same shade of brown eyes as Dad. Maybe that brown with a touch of gold was a Lewis family trait.

Matthew snapped me out of my fantasy when he put a hand on my shoulder, turned me toward him, and said, "I'm so happy for you, El."

And he was. He knew that while he and Mom were my family along with half the town of Williams-bridge, some part of me had always longed for some-thing more—perhaps for the sense of heritage that Edna had with her family.

Of course, I knew in that moment that even if I had a million cousins, I would always need Matthew. Possibly more than anyone else. But I wasn't about to tell him that.

"I've always wanted to go to Maine," he said quietly.

"Really?"

He nodded and grinned.

"Would you like to go with me—I mean, someday when I go?" I felt my cheeks getting warm and looked down, praying he hadn't noticed. "Just—it's supposed to be really beautiful there."

"Yes. Really beautiful."

I looked back up into his smiling eyes. "So . . . is that a yes?"

"That's a yes."

"Good."

"Good."

"What are you two talking about over there?" Mom asked, getting up to poke at the fire.

Matthew chuckled and gave me a sideways glance.

I nudged him with my elbow. "Our next adventure."

Edna's Honey-Butter Rolls (Eloise's Favorite!)

(makes 8 generous pieces—yeasty, sweet, and moist)

Ingredients:

1 cup milk

2 tablespoons butter

¼ cup honey

1 packet instant yeast

1 large egg, beaten

1 teaspoon sea salt

2 ¼ cups flour (or a bit more)

Topping:

4 tablespoons soft butter

2 tablespoons honey

Pinch of sea salt

1. Set the oven at 400 and grease 8 muffin cups.

2. Warm the milk just slightly in a saucepan and add the butter; stir together so that butter melts into milk.

3. Put the yeast and the honey into a large mixing bowl. (You can mix by hand or with a mixer.)

4. Add the warm milk mixture to the bowl and stir.

5. Add the salt and beaten egg.

6. Mix in about half of the flour.

7. Slowly add the remaining flour a little at a time—until the dough comes away from the sides of the bowl. (It will still be a bit sticky.)

8. Flour your hands and roll the dough into 8 balls of the same size; put into prepared muffin cups. Remember you can add a bit more flour if the dough is too sticky.

9. Cover and let rise for 10 minutes.

10. Bake about 15 minutes, until a knife inserted into a roll comes out clean (They'll be lightly browned.)

11. While the bread is piping hot, put a small dollop of honey butter onto each and let it melt down over the top. Serve warm with extra honey butter and a hot cup of tea or a bowl of soup!

Author's Note

I'd love to hear your thoughts on my books, the story-lines, and anything else that you'd like to comment on —reader feedback is very important to me. My contact information, along with some other helpful links, is listed on the next page. If you'd like to be on my list of "folks to contact" with updates, release and sales notifications, etc.... just shoot me an email and let me know. Thanks for reading!

Also...

... if you're looking for more great reads, Summer Prescott Books publishes several popular series by outstanding Cozy Mystery authors.

Contact Summer Prescott Books Publishing

Twitter: @summerprescott1

Bookbub: https://www.bookbub.com/authors/summer-prescott

Blog and Book Catalog: http://summerprescottbooks.com

Email: summer.prescott.cozies@gmail.com

YouTube: https://www.youtube.com/channel/UCngKNUkDdWuQ5k7-Vkfrp6A

And…be sure to check out the Summer Prescott Cozy Mysteries fan page and Summer Prescott Books Publishing Page on Facebook – let's be friends!

To download a free book, and sign up for our fun and exciting newsletter, which will give you opportunities to win prizes and swag, enter contests, and be the first to know about New Releases, click here: http://summerprescottbooks.com